This book belongs to

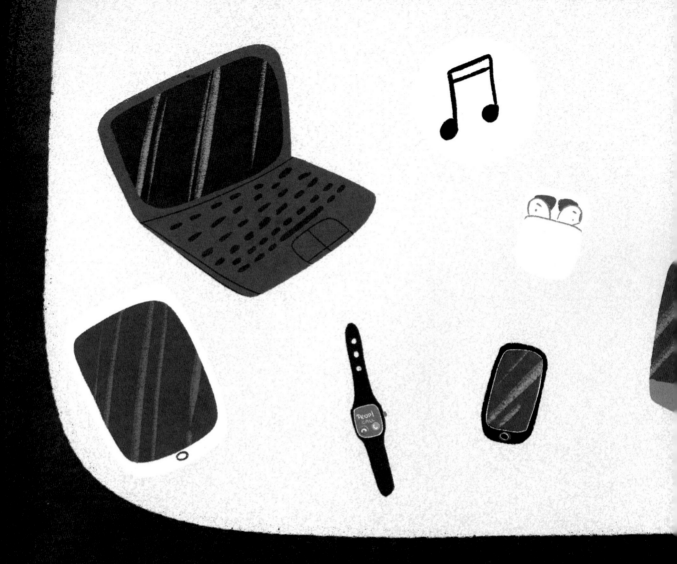

This book is dedicated to my children — Mikey, Kobe, and Jojo.

978-1-953399-11-3 Printed and bound in the USA. GrowGrit.co

The Apple logo is a trademark of Apple, Inc.

The Pixar logo is a trademark of Walt Disney Company.

Steve Jobs

By Mary Nhin

Illustrated by
Yuliia Zolotova

When my parents adopted me, they didn't realize their son would change the world.

But first, I had to develop my passions and overcome many obstacles.

I frequently helped my father in his workshop. He taught me many of his skills, including woodwork, electronics, and mechanics.

I fell in love with it. I could spend hours studying and practicing in our garage.

Hey Steve, grab me that hammer! Would ya?

My first obstacle was school. I struggled to pay attention and became bored easily. Oftentimes, I behaved very badly. This made it hard for me to make friends. I often felt sad and lonely. But I tried to keep my head up.

During this time, I made a great friend that would change my life forever. His name was Steve Wozniak. He was brilliant. We not only shared the same name, but also a common interest in technology and electronics.

I knew I wanted to change the world, but I needed to be brave. When I was thirteen, I mustered up the courage to call one of the biggest computer companies to ask for computer parts. From that one courageous step, I received an internship at Hewlett-Packard where I would continue my love of electronics.

One of the recurring challenges I faced was that I didn't have much money. So I collected Coke bottles and exchanged them for money.

Eventually, I got a job at Atari, a game development company.

Outside of work, I spent a lot of time with my friend, Steve. He would often show me what he was working on. One day, he showed me a new project he was working on. I immediately knew that Steve had created something special.

I persuaded him to go into business with me to turn his design into a computer that we could sell to people. We named our product the Apple I.

We started a company and named it Apple Computer Company. At first, we worked in my family's home kitchen, but then we moved it into the garage.

We got our first order of fifty units. Boy, were we happy!

But we were faced with a new obstacle. We didn't have any money to produce the order. So Steve and I sold our most precious belongings.

I couldn't believe it. By the age of twenty-three, I had made over a million dollars!

As the company grew, some of my co-workers and I argued over the direction for Apple. For a time, I was no longer working with the beloved company I created. I was very sad about it.

It was my biggest challenge yet. But I wouldn't let that deter me.

Instead, I turned my attention to other projects. I helped to create Pixar, a computer animation studio. We released the hit movies Toy Story, Bug's Life, and Finding Nemo.

Have you seen any of them?

When the opportunity arose, I went back to Apple. I was so happy to be back with my company!

We began to create groundbreaking products for people all around the world to use.

One of those inventions was a revolutionary mobile phone unlike any other. Back then, mobile phones were clunky and they had a plastic, tiny keyboard. They were called smart phones, but the problem was they were not very smart.

I wanted to change that.

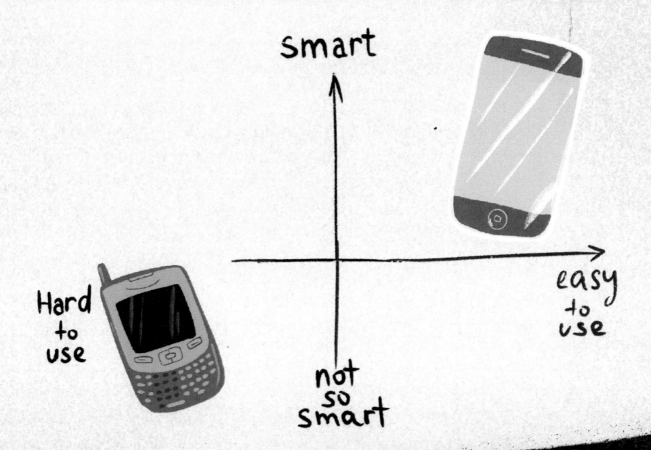

So we reinvented the mobile phone. We got rid of all of the buttons and just made a giant touchscreen. On our phone, people could browse the Internet, access emails, make phone calls, and listen to music. We called it the iPhone.

We also created the iPod, iPad, iMac, iWatch, iTunes, and AirPods.

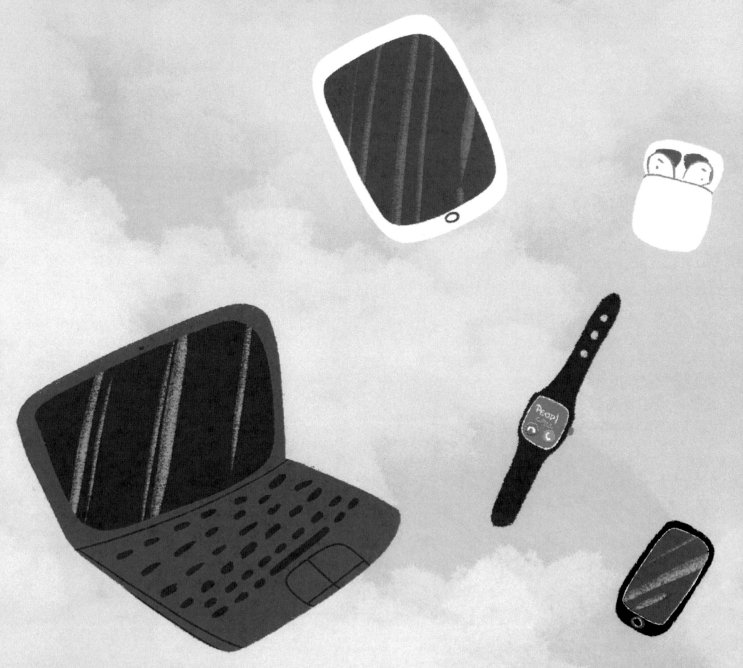

TIMELINE

1976 - Co-founds Apple Computer Company

1984 - Presents the 128k Apple Macintosh personal computer

1985 - Leaves Apple due to problems with other executives. In the same year, Steve is awarded the National Medal of Technology.

1986 - Creates Pixar

1997 - Returns to Apple

2001 - Presents the iPod

2003 - Apple launches iTunes

2004 - Undergoes cancer surgery

2007 - Apple launches the iPhone. In the same year, Steve is recognized as the most powerful person in business.

2010 - Apple launches the iPad

2011 - Resigns from Apple CEO position

2012 - Steve is given the Edison Achievement Award for his innovation.

minimovers.tv

 @marynhin @GrowGrit
#minimoversandshakers

Mary Nhin   Grow Grit

Ninja Life Hacks

83524107R00021